To Jen, Chris, and Liam

I Like to Read® books, created by award-winning
picture book artists as well as talented newcomers,
instill confidence and the joy of reading in new readers.

We want to hear every new reader say, "I like to read!"

Visit our website for flash cards, activities, and more about the series:
www.holidayhouse.com/ILiketoRead
#ILTR

This book has been officially leveled by using the
F&P Text Level Gradient™ Leveling System.

Copyright © 2020 by Steve Henry
All Rights Reserved
HOLIDAY HOUSE is registered in the U.S. Patent and Trademark Office.
Printed and bound in July 2020 at Tien Wah Press, Johor Bahru, Malaysia.
The artwork was created with watercolor, ink, acrylic paint,
and torn paper on 300 lb. hot press watercolor paper.

www.holidayhouse.com
First Edition
1 3 5 7 9 10 8 6 4 2

This book has been officially leveled by using the F&P Text Level Gradient™ Leveling System.

Library of Congress Cataloging-in-Publication Data is available.

ISBN 978-0-8234-4600-1

SNOW IS FUN

Steve Henry

I Like to Read®

HOLIDAY HOUSE • NEW YORK

Snow falls.

Snow is white.

Snow is quiet.

Snow falls and falls.

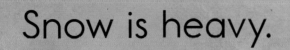

Snow is heavy.

Bird falls.

Friends try to help.

But birds can fly.

Snow is fun.

Snow is fun with friends.